Worm looks at Frog's feet.

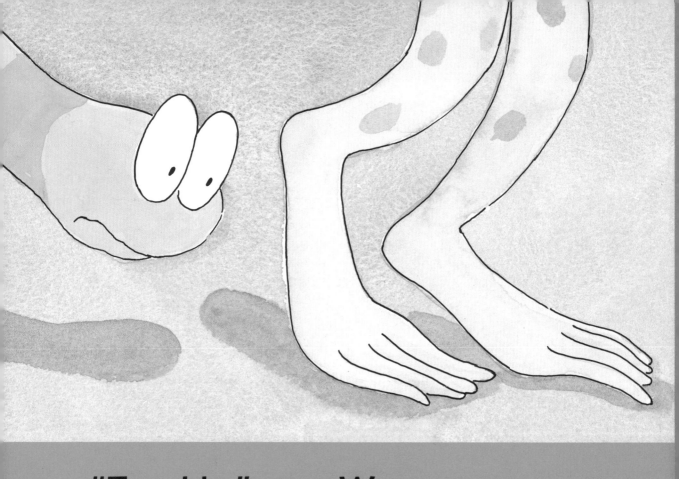

"Too big," says Worm.

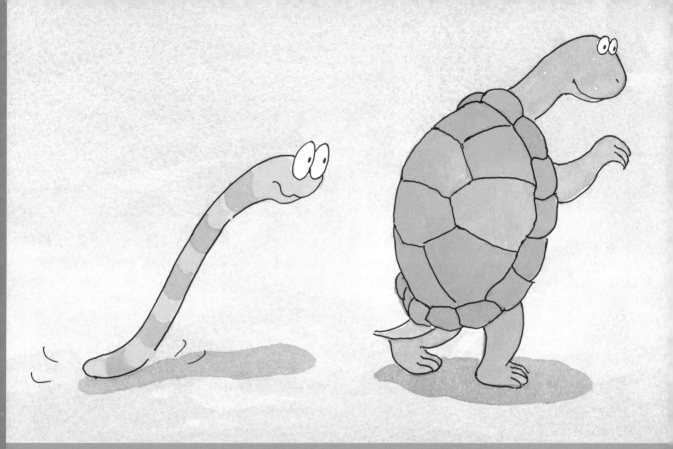

Worm looks at Turtle's shell.

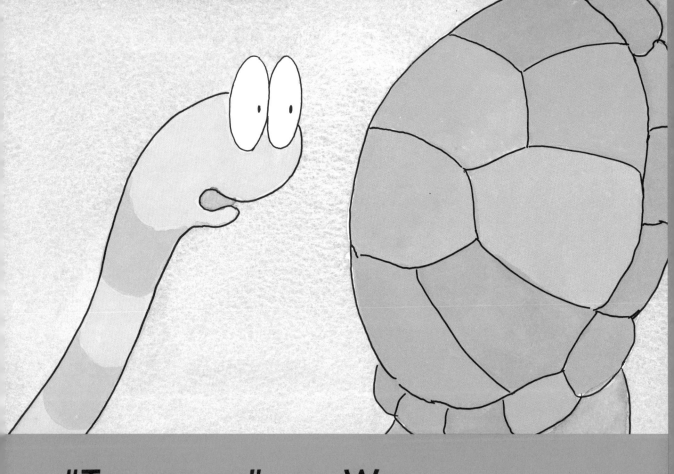

"Too green," says Worm.

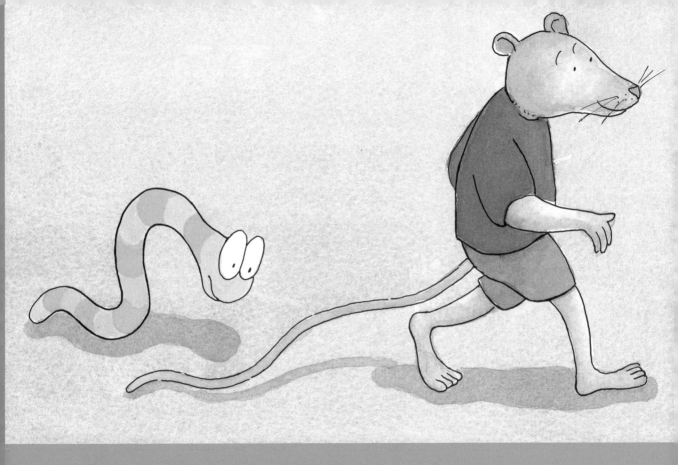

Worm looks at Rat's tail.

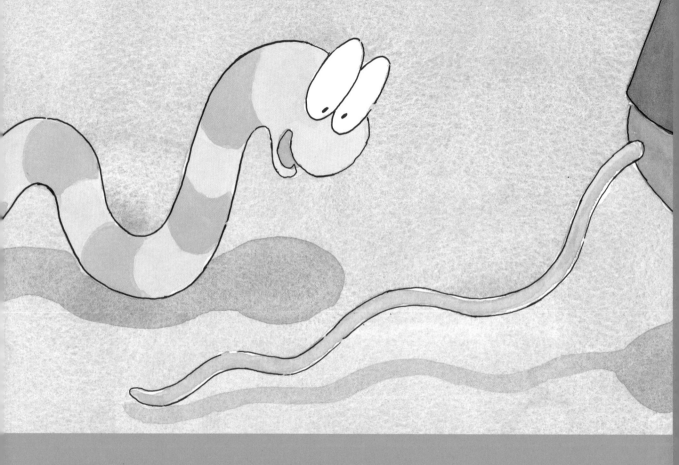

"Too long," says Worm.

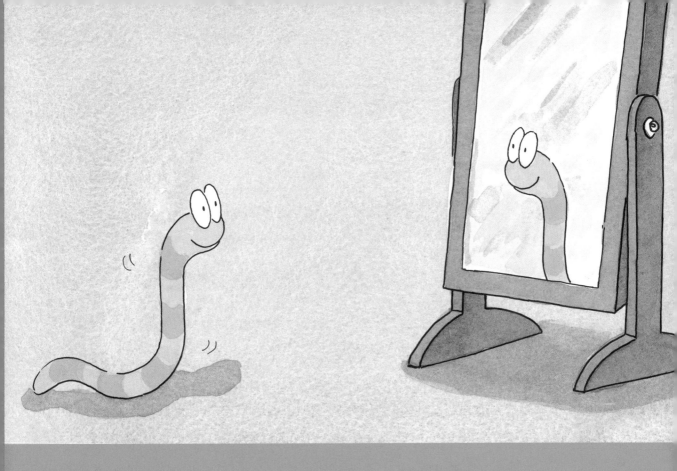

Worm looks at Worm.

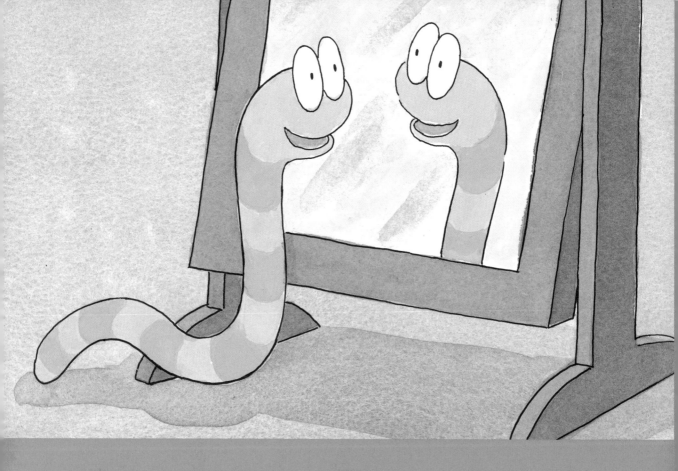

"Just right," says Worm.